The Twelve Days of Kindergarten

A Counting Book

written by
Deborah Lee Rose

illustrated by
Carey Armstrong-Ellis

HARRY N. ABRAMS, INC., PUBLISHERS

Kindergar
Room

On the first day of Kindergarten, my teacher gave to me

the whole alphabet from A to Z.

2 On the second day of Kindergarten,
my teacher gave to me
TWO picture books
and the whole alphabet from A to Z.

3 On the third day of Kindergarten,
my teacher gave to me
THREE pencils,
two picture books,
and the whole alphabet from A to Z.

4 On the fourth day of Kindergarten,
my teacher gave to me
FOUR puzzle shapes,
three pencils,
two picture books,
and the whole alphabet from A to Z.

5 On the fifth day of Kindergarten,
my teacher gave to me
FIVE gold stars!
Four puzzle shapes,
three pencils,
two picture books,
and the whole alphabet from A to Z.

6 On the sixth day of kindergarten,
my teacher gave to me
SIX fish for feeding,
five gold stars!
Four puzzle shapes,
three pencils,
two picture books,
and the whole alphabet from A to Z.

7 On the seventh day of Kindergarten,
my teacher gave to me
SEVEN stacks for sorting,

six fish for feeding,

five gold stars!

Four puzzle shapes,

three pencils,

two picture books,

and the whole alphabet from A to Z.

On the eighth day of Kindergarten,
my teacher gave to me
EIGHT beads for stringing,
seven stacks for sorting,
six fish for feeding,
five gold stars!
Four puzzle shapes,
three pencils,
two picture books,
and the whole alphabet from A to Z.

9 On the ninth day of Kindergarten,
my teacher gave to me
NINE blocks for building,
eight beads for stringing,
seven stacks for sorting,
six fish for feeding,
five gold stars!
Four puzzle shapes,
three pencils,
two picture books,
and the whole alphabet from A to Z.

10 On the tenth day of kindergarten,
my teacher gave to me
TEN coins for counting,
nine blocks for building,
eight beads for stringing,
seven stacks for sorting,
six fish for feeding,
five gold stars!
Four puzzle shapes,
three pencils,
two picture books,
and the whole alphabet from A to Z.

Children's Museum

11 On the eleventh day of Kindergarten,
my teacher gave to me
ELEVEN seeds for planting,
ten coins for counting,
nine blocks for building,
eight beads for stringing,
seven stacks for sorting,
six fish for feeding,
five gold stars!
Four puzzle shapes,
three pencils,
two picture books,
and the whole alphabet from A to Z.

12 On the twelfth day of Kindergarten,
my teacher gave to me
TWELVE eggs for hatching,
eleven seeds for planting,
ten coins for counting,
nine blocks for building,
eight beads for stringing,
seven stacks for sorting,
six fish for feeding,

five gold stars!
Four puzzle shapes,
three pencils,
two picture books,

today's word:
serenity

and the whole alphabet from A to Z!

To Mom and Pop, who always said I was a weird kid, but seemed to be okay with that.
—C. A. E.

To my favorite teachers, who give so much.
—D. L. R.

ACKNOWLEDGMENTS
Thanks to my family for putting up with my whining, and special thanks to Laaren Brown,
who was always ready to offer friendship and advice even when she didn't have to.
—C. A. E.

Library of Congress Cataloging-in-Publication Data

Rose, Deborah Lee.
The twelve days of kindergarten / by Deborah Lee Rose; illustrated by
Carey Armstrong-Ellis.
       p. cm.
Summary: A cumulative counting verse in which a child enumerates items
in the kindergarten classroom, from the whole alphabet, A to Z, to
twelve eggs for hatching.
  ISBN 0-8109-4512-6
  1. Kindergarten—Juvenile poetry. [1. Kindergarten—Poetry. 2.
American poetry. 3. Counting.] I. Armstrong-Ellis, Carey, ill. II. Title.

LB1167.R67 2003
372.21'8—dc21
                                              2002155970

10 9 8 7 6 5

Harry N. Abrams, Inc.
100 Fifth Avenue
New York, N.Y. 10011
www.abramsbooks.com

Abrams is a subsidiary of

LA MARTINIÈRE
GROUPE